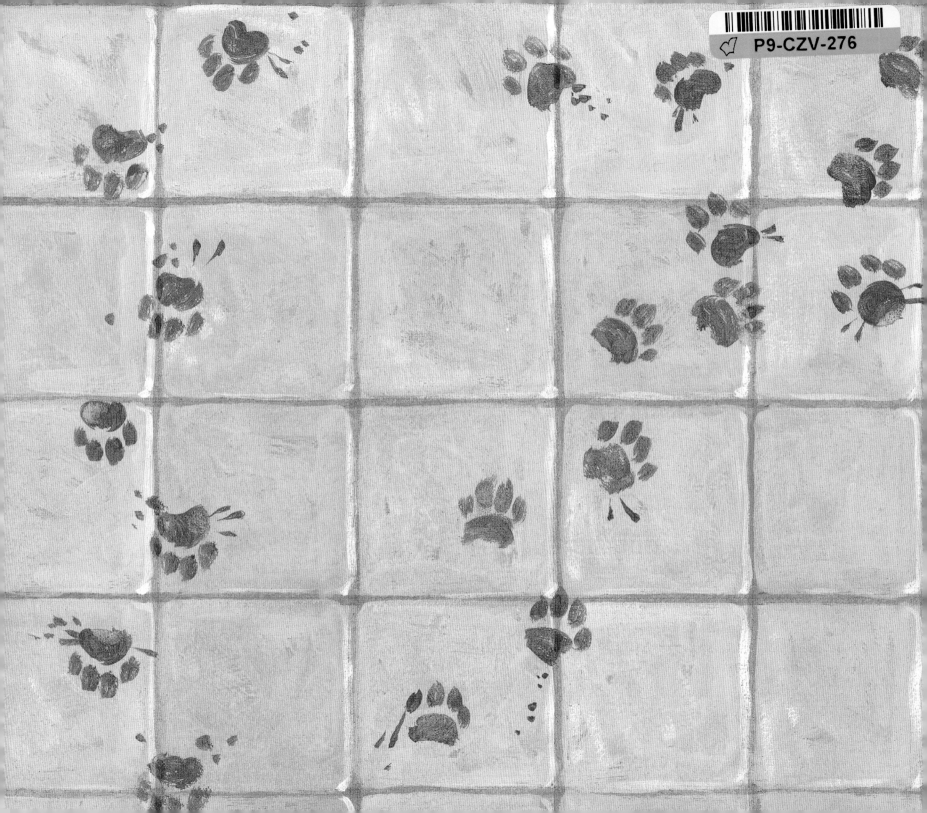

Andrew Clements
DOGKU

ILLUSTRATED BY TIM BOWERS

SIMON & SCHUSTER BOOKS FOR YOUNG READERS · New York · London · Toronto · Sydney

There on the back steps,
the eyes of a hungry dog.
Will she shut the door?

First food, then a bath.
The food was a lot more fun.
Still, it all feels good.

Morning brings children.
Hugs, licks, barking, and laughing.
Warmer than sunshine.

A dog needs a name.
Rags? Mutt? Pooch? No, not Rover.
Mooch. Yes, Mooch! Perfect.

Loud, fast, and crazy.
Food, coats, then the front door slams.
Mooch hates the school bus.

First, "Arf, arf!" Then, "Woof!"
Soon, "Arf, arf!" Then, "Woof! Woof, woof!"
Mooch has nice neighbors.

Nose out the window,
ears flapping, hair pushed straight back.
Adventures in smell.

The house is quiet.
No kids, no mom, and no food.
What's a dog to do?

Chew on dirty socks.
Roll around in week-old trash.
Ahhh . . . that's much better.

Squirrel sits in tree.
Mooch sits below, looking up.
Who has more patience?

Sun all morning long.
A deep, cool drink of water.
Shade all afternoon.

Scratch, sniff, eat, yawn, nap.
Dreams of rabbits and running.
Could life be sweeter?

The sound of children—
that's what was missing all day.
Mooch loves the school bus.

Family meeting.
There are words and words and words.
Did someone say "pound"?

Dad puts on his coat.
And then the sound of a car.
It doesn't look good.

It's the car again.
And then footsteps at the door.
Will this be good-bye?

A new doggy bed!
Food, a bowl, a squeaky toy!
Mooch has found his home.

· · · · Author's Note · · · ·

Vast ocean of words—
I am almost drowned again.
A haiku floats by.

Ever feel like there are so, *so* many words? And how could *I* ever put some
together and make a poem? That's when a haiku can seem like a lifeboat.
A haiku is so simple—only 17 syllables, 5/7/5. And who can resist trying to write one?
Not me. I got hooked on haiku a long time ago.
So here's another haiku about haiku writing:

In the wide garden,
I am dizzy with flowers.
I choose a small vase.

That's what a haiku is like—like a small vase, a small container. Choosing a small
container can help you pick the perfect words and arrange them just right.
And why did I write this picture book using haiku? Because a picture book is also a small
container—not many pages, not many words. Adorable dog + haiku = Dogku. Simple.

Andrew Clements

For Syd Lucey—friend, neighbor, and dedicated teacher
—A. C.

To Scott Jones
—T. B.

SIMON & SCHUSTER BOOKS FOR YOUNG READERS · An imprint of Simon & Schuster
Children's Publishing Division · 1230 Avenue of the Americas, New York, New York 10020 · Text
copyright © 2007 by Andrew Clements · Illustrations copyright © 2007 by Tim Bowers · All rights
reserved, including the right of reproduction in whole or in part in any form. · SIMON & SCHUSTER BOOKS FOR
YOUNG READERS is a trademark of Simon & Schuster, Inc. · Book design by Jessica Sonkin · The text for this
book is set in Hank BT. · The illustrations for this book are rendered in oil paint on canvas. · Manufactured in
China · 10 9 8 7 6 5 4 3 2 1 · Library of Congress Cataloging-in-Publication Data · Clements, Andrew, 1949–
Dogku / Andrew Clements ; illustrations by Tim Bowers. — 1st ed. · p. cm. · ISBN-13: 978-0-689-85823-9
ISBN-10: 0-689-85823-X · 1. Haiku, American. 2. Children's poetry, American. 3. Dogs—Juvenile
poetry. · I. Bowers, Tim, ill. I. Title. · PS3553.L3957D64 2006 · 811'.54—dc22 · 2006003691

first edition

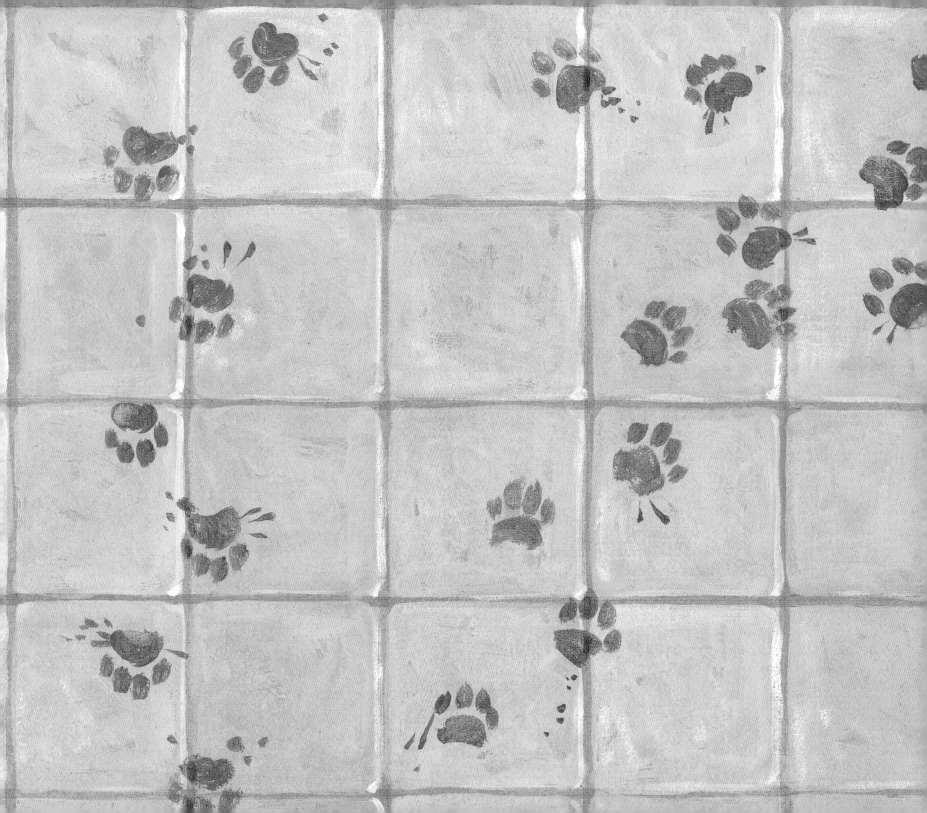